This book belongs to

_____

VOLUME
15

HIAWATHA'S
KIND HEART

WALT DISNEY FUN-TO-READ LIBRARY

A BANTAM BOOK
TORONTO • NEW YORK • LONDON • SYDNEY • AUCKLAND

Hiawatha's Kind Heart   A Bantam Book/January 1986   All rights reserved.   Copyright © 1986 Walt Disney Productions.   This book may not be reproduced, in whole or in part, by mimeograph or any other means.

ISBN 0-553-05592-5

Published simultaneously in the United States and Canada.   Bantam Books are published by Bantam Books, Inc.   Its trademark, consisting of the words "Bantam Books" and the portrayal of a rooster, is Registered in U.S. Patent and Trademark Office and in other countries.   Marca Registrada.   Bantam Books, Inc., 666 Fifth Avenue, New York, New York 10103.   Printed in the United States of America   0 9 8 7 6 5 4 3 2 1

It was a big day in the Indian town
where Little Hiawatha lived. The braves were
going on a great hunt.

"I wish I could hunt with the braves," Hiawatha said.

"It is hard to be a brave," said the chief. "You must be able to live alone in the forest. You must be able to hunt for your food."

Hiawatha nodded. Then he walked quietly into his tent.

"I could do all that," thought Hiawatha. "I will show the chief that I am ready to be a brave."

So Hiawatha got his bow and arrows. Then he went outside.

"Where are you going, Little Hiawatha?" his mother asked.

"I am going into the forest. I will learn to be a brave," he said. "I can find my own food. I will show the chief that I can be a great hunter."

Hiawatha paddled his small canoe across the deep lake. On the far side of the lake was a big forest. "That looks like a good place to hunt," he thought. He paddled his canoe to the shore.

There he saw a deer.
"How lucky I am!" thought Little Hiawatha.
"Not every brave who hunts can find a deer
so soon."

Hiawatha fit an arrow to his bow. He aimed it at the deer.

Just then the deer lifted its head. It
looked straight at Hiawatha.

Hiawatha looked back at the deer. He could not shoot. He put away his bow and arrow. Then he watched the deer run away.

Hiawatha started walking through the
forest. He began to feel a bit hungry.

Soon he saw a mother quail and her five small round baby quails. They were walking toward a bush full of ripe red berries.

"A nice fat quail would taste very good,"
Hiawatha thought. He lifted his bow. He fit an
arrow to it.

Just then the mother quail saw him. She
called to her babies. She covered them with
her wings.

Hiawatha looked at the mother quail. How brave she was! He just could not shoot her. Without her, the baby quails would die.

"Squawk, squawk," Hiawatha heard from the berry bush. A father quail seemed to say that there were plenty of berries for all. So Hiawatha ate a few. Then he put some away to save for later.

Little Hiawatha then went farther into the forest.

Soon he heard the chatter of squirrels ahead. He saw a baby squirrel running up a tree.

Hiawatha lifted his bow again. Just as he
was about to shoot, he heard a rustling in the
tree. He looked up. On a high branch he saw
a father and mother squirrel. They were afraid
for their baby.

Hiawatha threw down his bow and arrow.
He waved to the squirrels to show them that
he would not shoot their baby.

The baby squirrel came down the tree.
All three squirrels offered to share their nuts
with Hiawatha.

Both Hiawatha and the baby squirrel ate
until they were full. Then Hiawatha put some
nuts away to save for later.

The sun began to set. "I had better find a place to sleep," Hiawatha thought. He snuggled between the big roots of a tree. The baby squirrel curled up beside him. They both went right to sleep.

In the middle of the night Hiawatha woke
up. Rain was falling. Hiawatha was cold and
wet. Suddenly he felt a wet nose pushing at
his arm. There was the deer he had met
at the lake.

The deer led him to some leafy bushes.
They curled up together under the heavy
leaves. There they could stay warm and dry.

When morning came, the rain had
stopped. Hiawatha rubbed the sleep from
his eyes. He waved good-bye to the deer
and went on his way.

Across the clearing, Hiawatha spotted a
rabbit. It was hopping off into the bushes.
Hiawatha went to follow it.

Behind the bushes he found another
rabbit. This one had its foot caught in a trap.
The first rabbit was trying to help. Hiawatha
thought how good rabbit stew would taste.

He aimed his bow at the rabbits. They
turned to look at him. They were so afraid,
their whiskers shook.

Hiawatha's eyes filled with tears. He could not shoot the rabbits. Instead, Hiawatha opened the trap. The rabbits were so happy! They danced around Hiawatha. Then they hopped away. Hiawatha followed them.

But suddenly he stopped. Before him
stood a busy old beaver.

Hiawatha had always wanted a soft,
warm, beaver skin hat. The old beaver saw
Hiawatha. He thought Hiawatha wanted to
play. "I am too busy to play with you," he
seemed to say.

Well, Hiawatha could not shoot the busy beaver. He took out all his arrows. He broke every one of them across his knee. He threw away his bow for good.

Then Hiawatha went to work. He pulled
down tree branches. He carried them to the
river. Hiawatha helped the beavers build
their dam.

After a while, Hiawatha grew tired. He waved good-bye to his new friends. He walked slowly along the river. Then he stopped to eat berries from a giant bush.

All at once Hiawatha heard a warning call from the quail. His rabbit friends were pointing their ears toward the far side of the bush.

There stood a great big bear! This was <u>his</u> berry bush. These were <u>his</u> berries. The bear growled. Then he jumped at Hiawatha.

Hiawatha did not stop to think. He raced along the river. The bear was close behind him.

The squirrels in the treetop threw nuts at the bear. But the bear did not stop. He kept running after Hiawatha.

The beaver had heard the bear crashing through the forest. He chewed busily at a great big tree trunk. Then he waited until the bear ran by.

As the bear passed, the beaver took one last bite of the tree trunk. With his tail, he gave it a push. *Crash!* It fell right on that mean old bear!

Hiawatha was safe! He thanked all
his forest friends. Then he ran all the
way through the forest, back to the lake.

Little Hiawatha climbed into his canoe.
Then he paddled home to the Indian town.
He went as fast as his arms could paddle.

His mother and the chief were waiting
for him there.

"How was the hunt?" they asked.

Hiawatha told them how the forest
animals had helped him and how they had
become his friends.

"You are very wise, my son," said the chief. "Every true brave knows that a kind heart is often better than a strong arm."

And Hiawatha was proud of himself. At last he had become a true Indian brave.